HORRIBLE HARRY
and the Stolen Cookie

HORRIBLE HARRY
and the Stolen Cookie

BY SUZY KLINE
PICTURES BY AMY WUMMER

SCHOLASTIC INC.

ISBN 978-0-545-67923-7

12 11 10 9 8 7 6 5 4 3   15 16 17 18/0

Printed in the U.S.A.   40

First Scholastic printing, December 2013

Set in New Century Schoolbook LT Std

Dedicated to my beautiful granddaughter
Gabrielle Lauren DeAngelis,
who collects food for the soup kitchen
and makes stuffed animals
for children in the hospital.
I love you, Gabby!
Grandma Sue

Special appreciation to . . .

My patient husband, Rufus, who listened to me many times about the story and made valuable suggestions; my precious granddaughter Mikenna, who helped me write about the chocolate chip cookie; my loving daughter Emily, who makes the best chocolate chip cookies; Wheelock Elementary School in Medfield, Massachusetts; George Washington Elementary School in White Plains, New York; and all the other caring schools I visited who raised funds for charities.

And a special thank you to my hardworking editor, Leila Sales, for her critical questions and very helpful comments.

Contents

The Super Cookie

My name is Doug and I'm in third grade. I write stories about my best friend, Harry, and all the horrible things he loves. I've written about an earwig, green slime, a dungeon, a burnt wiener, vultures, and even dead fish.

This story is different.

It's about a chocolate chip cookie.

Not a regular one. A *super* cookie. I needed it to have special powers. I had to use it to stop Harry from doing the most horrible thing he had ever planned to do.

What was that horrible thing? And did the super cookie work?

I'll tell you all about it.

Not a Normal
Harry Day

It started on Monday morning before
school. Harry got out of his grandma's
red truck as usual, closed the door, and
then did something very *un*usual.

Harry did not run down the ramp to
the playground.

He just stood there, watching us play
kickball.

I waved to him. "You can be on my
team!" I shouted. I rolled the red rubber

ball over the plate. Song Lee kicked it high into right field, then dashed to first base.

Well, Harry didn't join us. He just sat down at the top of the ramp and crossed his arms. He didn't even say *yahoo* when Song Lee touched home plate and scored a home run!

I could tell right away that today was not a normal Harry day.

Later in the morning, our class went to the library. Our librarian, Mrs. Michaelsen, came over to Harry. "I have a brand-new book for you," she said.

I shivered when I saw the cover. It had a picture of a big hairy tarantula with eight eyeballs!

"No thanks," Harry said, and he shuffled over to the nearest table and sat down.

I made a beeline for Harry.

"What's going on?" I asked as I sat next to him. "You love creepy books like that."

"I can't talk about it, Doug," he mumbled.

"Why not?" I said. "That's what friends are for. You talk about things, and maybe they can help."

"Not with this," he replied.

"With what?" I asked.

"It's private!" Harry insisted.

Whoa, I thought. This was not a normal Harry day.

At noon, things got worse.

Harry wasn't in the hot lunch line.

"Hey," I said. "Where are you going?"

Harry pointed to Room 3B's lunch table. He had a lunchbox in his hand.

I grabbed my tray of hot food and followed him.

"You always eat hot lunch on sausage day," I said. "What's up?"

"Nothing," he answered.

"Want my broccoli?" I asked. I knew Harry loved that smelly vegetable.

Harry shook his head.

I dangled a sausage link in front of his face. "Want a juicy bite?"

"Nope," Harry answered. Then he reached for his peanut butter sandwich.

We didn't say another word. We

just ate our lunches. Everyone else at Room 3B's table was busy talking about the third grade's annual Sharing and Caring Tag Sale. It was coming up on Thursday.

"Which charity do you want to earn money for?" Mary asked. "Miss Mackle said we get to vote after lunch."

"I know who I'm voting for," Sidney replied. "The animal shelter. They save lots of dogs from the death chamber."

"It's not called a death chamber," Mary corrected. "Dogs are put to sleep."

"It's the same thing," Sid insisted. "It's not fair. Animal shelters need money to keep dogs alive."

"Well," Mary said, "I'm voting for the Girl Scouts! That's a very caring group. I know because I am a Girl Scout. We col- lect food for community soup kitchens,

and we make things for nursing homes."

Dexter raised his hand and pretended to write in the air. "I'm doing a write-in ballot. I'm voting for the EFC!"

"EFC?" Mary questioned. "That sounds like KFC."

Dexter chuckled. "Well," he said, "Elvis did like fried chicken, but that's not what EFC means. It's the Elvis Fan Club!"

"That's not a charity," Mary replied.

Dexter made a fist. "Bummer," he mumbled.

Harry finally broke his silence. "Don't you know charity begins at home?" he snapped. "Granddad says that all the time."

Mary carefully set her tuna salad sandwich back in its plastic container. "Harry Spooger," she said slowly, "we are *not* going to earn money so we can spend it on ourselves."

"I don't see why not!" Harry insisted.

No, today was *definitely* not a normal Harry day.

Dash for Cash

That afternoon, we lined up for gym class. Usually Harry bolts for the door. He likes to be first.

Today he didn't seem to care. He just went to the end of the line.

Man, I thought, *Harry's still sulking!*

When we got to the gym, Mr. Deltoid had a surprise for us. He was holding a big sign that said DASH FOR CASH.

Harry stood on his tiptoes to read it.

"Boys and girls," Mr. Deltoid said, "as you know, the third graders at South School are earning money this week for the charities of their choice. I thought you might like to continue that money-earning spirit in gym today. See this poster?"

Everyone reread the words DASH FOR CASH and nodded. Even Harry.

"Every time you run a lap, you earn one dollar."

Mr. Deltoid pointed to a white Monopoly-money bill taped to the bottom of the poster. "I'll keep track of your earnings. Ready?"

Harry started running in place.

"Go!" Mr. Deltoid shouted.

Harry took off like a roadrunner. He passed people one by one. When he got to the first corner of the gym and rounded the turn, Harry led the pack! I tried to catch up with him, but he was out of reach. Dexter was hot on his heels. Song Lee and Ida were tied for third. I could see their hair swaying back and forth.

"Hey, Harry!" I called out, breathing hard. "I knew you were fast, but not this fast!"

Dexter was humming an Elvis tune. "I'm feelin' it!" he said. "I'm running like a hound dog!" And then he sang, "'You ain't nuthin' but a hound dog,'" as he followed Harry around the next turn.

Harry looked over his shoulder at Dexter. They were side by side now. Harry gave Dex the thumbs-up sign. *Wow*, I thought, *Harry's back!*

Dexter kept bobbing his head to the tune of his Elvis song.

By the tenth lap, I was losing speed. When ZuZu and Sid passed me, I joined Mary in the rest station. She had been the first one to stop.

"Two laps, and I was done!" Mary held up two white one dollar bills. "How much did you earn, Doug?"

"Eleven," I said, a little out of breath.

Mary looked up and saw Harry round the gym again. "Harry acts like he's running for real money," she said.

I watched Harry as he finished another lap. When he got closer to me, he rubbed his fingers together and yelled, "Moolah moolah!"

Oh, no, I thought. Could Mary be right? Harry *was* at the end of the line when we got to gym. Could he see the money taped to the bottom of Mr. Deltoid's sign? It was a white bill from the Monopoly game, not a green dollar bill with George Washington's face on it.

I plopped on the gym floor next to Mary. One by one, other kids started joining us. They were pooped, too.

Finally, Dexter sat down with two yellow bills and a pink five.

But Harry was still running.

Mr. Deltoid clapped his hands. "Good job, guys!" he said. "Now that you're done, you can play ring toss, bean bag toss, or jump rope."

We all got up and chose our activities in the center of the gym.

"Stop when you're tired," Mr. Deltoid called to Harry.

Ten minutes later, Harry finally collapsed.

He was out of breath and dripping wet when the gym teacher handed him the cash he had earned. "Three yellow tens, one pink five, and two white ones," Mr. Deltoid said. "Congratulations,

Harry! You earned the most money!"

"Huh?" Harry's mouth dropped open. "This is . . . play . . . money," he gasped.

"You can keep it," Mr. Deltoid said. "You worked hard for it."

Harry stared at the thirty-seven dollars in his sweaty hand. Slowly he let the play money slide from his fingers onto the floor.

"Okay, kids," Mr. Deltoid shouted. "It's time to line up." Then he motioned for Harry to pick up his money.

He did, but when the teacher had his back turned, Harry threw all of it into the trash can.

Mary was right. Harry *was* dashing for real cash!

My question now was . . . why?

Why Harry Ran So Hard

The last hour of the day, Harry put his head down on his desk and stared at the floor. Everyone, including the teacher, thought that Harry was exhausted. After all, he had just run thirty-seven laps. But I knew better. Harry was bummed about the play money. I just didn't know why.

Miss Mackle went to the whiteboard and took out her red marker.

"As you know, we are having our Sharing and Caring Tag Sale on Thursday," she said. "I counted the votes while you were in gym, and I am happy to tell you which three charities will receive our donations. There were so many wonderful ones to choose from."

Lots of people started clapping when they read the names on the whiteboard.

ASPCA, the American Society for the Prevention of Cruelty to Animals.

UNICEF, the United Nations International Children's Emergency Fund.

GSUSA, Girl Scouts of the United States of America.

"Yes!" Mary blurted out.

"I want each of you to make a poster

for one of these charities tonight for homework," Miss Mackle said. "Please use their initials. You'll hang your poster on the front of your desk for our tag sale."

ZuZu was beaming. "Yahoo! UNICEF won! My great-grandmother lives in Lebanon, and she told me they help poor and sick children there."

"I voted for that charity, too," Song Lee added. "UNICEF helps children in Korea, and that's where I was born. My aunt Sun Yee told me UNICEF cleaned up the polluted water near our old house."

Miss Mackle smiled. "All right," she said. "Now, do any of you know what you will be selling at our tag sale?"

Ida spoke first. "Song Lee taught me

how to make friendship bracelets. We've made two dozen already!"

Song Lee held her hand up so we could see the one on her wrist. The multicolored strings were all braided together. "Do you think fifteen cents is fair?" she asked.

"It's worth at least a quarter," I said. Song Lee and Ida bounced up and down in their seats. They liked the price.

I shared next. "I'm bringing a box of used children's books. They're still good, though. Not one page is ripped out. And I'm not selling the books my brother scribbled in."

"Wonderful!" Miss Mackle replied.

"We can sell used things, but they should be in good condition."

"Can we bake something?" Mary asked. "I want to make challah rolls. I love braiding the dough before it goes into the oven."

"That's a great idea," Miss Mackle replied. "But all baked goods must be wrapped in foil or plastic for sanitary reasons. And that will make it easier for the children to take them home."

Mary nodded. "Oh, I will be sure to wrap each roll very carefully!"

I nudged Harry. He was still slouched over

his desk, and I wanted to cheer him up. "Hey, you could bake something, too. Your grandma could help." Grandma Spooger bakes cakes and cookies all the time. She runs a bakery business out of her own kitchen.

Harry sat up. "No, I can't ask her, Doug." He lowered his voice. "Grandma's stove broke down. She can't bake anything until she gets her oven fixed. We have to save every nickel and dime for the repair job. It's expensive!"

Oh boy, I thought. So *that* was the reason Harry ran so hard for cash. And why he couldn't afford a hot lunch on sausage day. Harry had a money problem.

"That's too bad," I said.

"Don't tell anyone," Harry whispered.

"Grandma says we shouldn't talk about our money problems."

"But . . . if you do talk about it, maybe someone could help," I whispered back.

"No! Just forget it, okay?" Harry insisted.

"Okay," I replied. "I won't mention your stove again."

I reluctantly sealed our pact with a knuckle tap. Then Harry went to get a drink of water.

After Harry had walked away, Mary

leaned over and said, "Did you just say 'stove'? We're getting a new one this week! It's going to be buttercup yellow to match our newly painted kitchen."

"Well, goody for you!" I snapped.

"What did I say?" Mary asked.

"Nothing, Mare. Forget it." I couldn't tell Mary about Harry's money problem. He had asked me to keep it private, and he trusted me.

The teacher stopped listing things on the whiteboard and turned around. "Please don't forget to take home notices for your parents about our Sharing and Caring Tag Sale on Thursday. And remember to use the charities' initials on your posters."

Everyone watched the teacher erase

most of the board. Only the initials of the charities were left. When I looked over at Harry, he was standing in the middle of the room, staring at the whiteboard.

ASPCA
UNICEF
GSUSA

Suddenly Harry rushed back to his seat. "I've got it!" he said.

"Got what?" I asked.

"My favorite charity!" Harry replied. "The GS fund!"

Mary cheered. "Yippee! Harry's going to help earn money for the Girl Scouts!"

Harry nodded. "Go GS!" he said, punching the air with his fist.

Why was Harry so excited to earn money for the Girl Scouts?

Harry raised his eyebrows. "GS . . . get it, Dougo?" he whispered. "Now I can *really* help Grandma!"

What was Harry up to?

The GS Fund

The next morning, after Grandma Spooger dropped Harry off at school, he raced down the ramp. He had a poster rolled up under his arm.

"I worked for two hours on my charity poster last night. Want to see it, Doug?"

Harry unrolled the chart paper. It had five words written in big block letters. Each of the letters had stick people sitting or hanging on it.

GIVE TO THE GS FUND!

"That's pretty cool," I said.

"Thanks, Dougo. See these guys hanging from the letters?" Harry asked. "They're stub people!"

I grinned. I loved those things. Harry made stub people out of anything he found on our classroom floor: pencil stubs, broken crayons, bent paper clips, and old erasers.

"I'm making a battalion of them," Harry continued. "I'll sell my stub people at our tag sale and split the profits fifty-fifty between the Girl Scouts and my own GS Fund."

"What do you mean, your *own* GS Fund?" I asked.

Harry cupped his hands around

my ear and whispered his answer. *"Grandma's Stove."*

"Your grandma's stove?" I repeated. "Wait a minute . . . you mean the GS Fund is not the Girl Scouts?"

Harry slowly nodded. "Charity begins at home," he explained.

"You can't do that!" I objected. "Everyone will think their donations are going to the Girl Scouts, and they won't be. That's false advertising! Besides, if anyone catches you, you could get in big trouble. People go to *jail* for stealing stuff!"

"I'm not stealing," Harry snapped. "I'm earning money for two good charities: the Girl Scouts and my grandmother!"

I gritted my teeth. "Harry, Grandma Spooger is not a charity!"

Harry stared at his poster. He wasn't listening to me anymore.

"Hey, Dougo," he said, "which stub person on my poster do you like best?"

"Harry!" I shouted. "You're being *stub*born!"

When the bell rang, Harry took off for the school door. "I can't wait to show Miss Mackle my poster!" he called out.

Harry was on a collision course.

I had to think of something to stop him!

Moolah Moolah

Thursday morning, Miss Mackle asked us to arrange our desks in a big U shape. She wanted all the students who visited our tag sale to see what we were selling.

I was still working on a plan to stop Harry. I moved my desk next to Harry's. I had to keep an eye on him.

Harry had one hundred stub people lined up in ten rows. I liked the General best. He was a big old eraser with an army hat made out of a brown crayon wrapper. Harry gouged out eyes and put bits of black crayon in the holes for pupils. He even bent a paper clip to give the General a silver mustache.

"Your stub people are awesome," I said.

"Thanks, Dougo." Harry grinned.

"How come you don't have a stub *girl*?" Mary asked.

"Actually, I do have one," Harry said. He lifted up a tall pencil stub with long yellow yarn hair. He had penned in two eyes on her eraser head. "Her name is Sue Per. Get it?"

Song Lee came over to admire it. "She's so cute!" she exclaimed. "Do you think Sue Per would like a bow in her hair?"

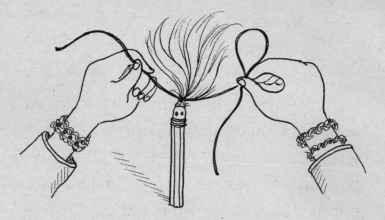

"Sure," Harry replied. We watched Song Lee tie a red string around Sue Per's yellow hair. The red bow added a lot. "Now she has a ponytail!" Song Lee giggled.

Mary clapped her hands. "You should have made more girls, Harry," she said. "Sue Per looks like a basketball player!"

"Trade you Sue Per for one of your bread rolls," he suggested.

"No, thanks," Mary replied. "It isn't a fair trade. My rolls are worth more than your stub people. And they're *challah* rolls, Harry. Not plain rolls."

I looked at Mary's desk. Each golden challah roll had a six-strand braid and was wrapped in clear plastic with a pink bow. She and her mom had made four dozen.

"If I charge fifty cents apiece for them," Mary said, "I'll earn twenty-four dollars for the Girl Scouts!"

"Well, I know I don't have fifty cents." Harry groaned. He reached into his pocket and pulled out a handful of dirty coins, one bottle cap, and some cat hair. "This is my life savings."

Mary rolled her eyes.

Harry tugged at my sleeve. "How much do you think I should charge for each stub person, Dougo?" he asked.

Mary answered right away, "A penny, maybe? But two cents for Sue Per."

"Very funny, Mare," Harry said.

Suddenly, an idea popped into my head. "I think your stub people are worth lots of money," I said.

Harry got a toothy smile. "You mean . . . lots of moolah moolah?"

"Yes! They're original art," I continued. "You should charge a dollar each."

"Whoa," Harry replied. "You think I could sell them for that much?"

Of course he couldn't. But I wasn't going to tell Harry that.

"Absolutely!" I said.

It was a perfect plan. If Harry couldn't sell his stub people, then he wouldn't have any money to steal! "Harry," I said, "one dollar is a bargain for those guys. Maybe more for the General."

Mary looked down at her poster.

I knew she didn't want Harry to see
her laughing. I felt bad having to fib to
Harry, but it was the only thing I could
come up with. I had to do something!

"Okay, one buck it is!" Harry said.
And he got busy making a sign that
said ONE DOLLAR EACH. He also added a
special price tag for the General. Five
dollars!

I had to look away. I was beginning
to feel guilty.

Harry tapped me on the shoulder.

"If I sell all of my stub people, I'll have about fifty smackeroos for Grandma's stove," he whispered.

I gritted my teeth. I didn't feel guilty anymore. I grabbed one of the books I was selling.

"See the title of this one?"

"That's *Curious George*," Harry replied. "I've read it lots of times."

I put my nose in Harry's face. "Remember the part where George goes to *jail*?"

Harry put two thumbs in the air. "Yeah! That's my favorite part, because George escapes!"

Harry was not getting my message. I just had to hope that he didn't make one single sale.

Sid's Warm Cookies

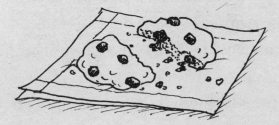

Just as we were about to begin our tag sale, Sidney burst into the room with a dog and cat poster under his arm. His stepdad was right behind him, carrying two big boxes. We could smell chocolate as soon as they entered the room.

"Sorry I'm late, guys," Sid said. "I was baking chocolate chip cookies. We just took them out of the oven this morning. Nothing like warm cookies!"

He had one in his hand. It was so soft and warm it broke into two pieces. I could see melted chocolate oozing out. Sidney quickly popped the cookie into his mouth. "I can't sell a broken one," he mumbled.

Harry frowned. A working oven was a sore subject for him.

As I watched Sidney eat that delicious broken cookie, I got another idea for a plan. It was a horrible thing to do to a friend. But if Harry was able to sell just one stub person, I would have to use it.

"They smell divine," Miss Mackle said.

"Well, Sid forgot a few things," Mr. LaFleur said. "He didn't tell me he needed something to sell at the fair

until early this morning. So that's why the cookies are warm."

Miss Mackle sighed. "Oh, that's too bad," she said. "Sidney, didn't you bring home the reminder notice on Monday?"

"I . . . forgot," Sid confessed. "I'm really sorry."

"He's going to bring home school notices from now on!" Mr. LaFleur said sternly. "And, do his homework on time. Right, Sid?"

"Right," Sid insisted. Then he taped his animal shelter poster to the front of his desk.

"Okay, guys. Good luck on your charity fair," Mr. LaFleur called out. He gave his stepson a kiss on the head and left.

Sid took the lid off one of the boxes. The chocolate chip cookies were each in a sealed plastic Baggie. It was torture not being able to eat one. They smelled even more chocolaty with the lid off the box.

Ida handed baby food jars to each of us. "These are for your money," she said. "I have lots more jars at home. My baby sister loves to eat."

Miss Mackle said, "Let's give Ida a big hand for washing them out and bringing them in." Everyone clapped for Ida.

"At the end of the day," Miss Mackle said, "you will dump your earnings into one of the three large mayonnaise jars on my desk."

Each one had a set of initials on it: ASPCA, GSUSA, or UNICEF.

We all nodded. Even Harry.

Then Harry showed me a brown leather coin purse he had inside his desk. "For my own GS fund. I'll take it home after school," he whispered.

I crossed my fingers that Harry wouldn't sell a single one of his over-priced stub people.

Kerplink! Kerplunk!

"Someone's at the door!" Sid shouted.

The first group that came into Room 3B was a fourth grade class. Our art teacher, Mrs. Mattalatta, was with them. "I love your posters!" she exclaimed. "They're so colorful!"

It wasn't long before we heard the sounds of the first few sales. Two kids bought chocolate chip cookies from Sid for thirty cents each.

Kerplink! Kerplunk! Sid dropped the change into his glass jar.

Mrs. Mattalatta bought two of Mary's braided challah rolls. *Kerplink! Kerplunk!* Mary proudly deposited the silver coins in her baby food jar.

"I'll get that *Curious George* book for my little brother," a fourth grade girl said as she handed me a quarter.

"Thanks!" I dropped the coin into my jar. My first sale! *Kerplink!*

Lots of the fourth grade girls gathered around Song Lee's and Ida's desks. "Oh . . . those bracelets are so cute!" a girl said.

"I love the colors! I'm getting two. One for each wrist!" said another.

Song Lee and Ida were busy handing out their braided string bracelets and depositing coins in their money jars. *Kerplink! Kerplunk! Kerplink! Kerplunk!* Just as quickly as they sold a batch, they brought out another from their box of reserves on the floor.

Harry sat at his desk, waiting. Two fourth grade boys stopped by and looked at the stub people. One picked up the General. "Cool," he said. Then he saw the five dollar price tag and walked away.

Harry got a long face.

Mrs. Mattalatta stopped by and admired Harry's work, too. "I'm going to do a stub people art lesson someday. They look like fun, Harry. What a good way to recycle old materials!"

Harry tried to smile, but Mrs. Mattalatta didn't buy one, either.

By the time the first class left, everyone had made a sale except Harry. His stub people were still lined up on his desk in ten rows. "I'm changing the price," Harry mumbled. "It's too much moolah moolah."

"Just remember it's original art," I said. I hoped he'd keep the price high.

Harry shook his head. "Nah, I gotta get real." And he crossed off ONE DOLLAR and wrote, SALE PRICE FIFTEEN CENTS. The General was a quarter.

"You're just charging fifteen cents?" I replied. "That's a *steal*!" And then right after I said that, I nodded to myself. That's what Harry was planning to do. Steal from the Girl Scouts!

The fifth grade group that came next bought lots of Harry's stub people.

They loved them. One tall boy bought
the General. He pretended to make him
talk as he stopped by my book display.
He picked up *The Book of Lists* and said
to me in his General voice, "I like this
book. It has lots of facts in it. Maybe

there will even be some about the army."
And then the tall boy made the General
jump on top of the book.

"Thanks," I said, dropping his quarter into my jar.

Harry was busy collecting silver
coins for his stub people. He dropped
some into his money jar, and some into
the brown leather coin purse in his
desk. I couldn't stand watching him zip
that thing open and closed.

I knew I had to use my horrible plan.
It was just a matter of when.

My Horrible Chocolate Chip Cookie Plan

As the afternoon rolled on, Harry sold all his stub people. The second graders especially loved them. "I can't believe it, Dougo!" Harry exclaimed. "I sold my entire battalion of men!"

"Yes, you did," I said. I wasn't smiling.

Harry lowered his voice. "I earned fifteen dollars and ten cents, Dougo. Seven dollars and fifty-five cents for the Girl Scouts and seven dollars and fifty-five cents for my GS Fund. That's fair and square."

That's it! I thought. It was time to put my horrible plan into action. "Hey, Harry. We've been smelling chocolate all day. Do you want to chip in with me and buy a cookie from Sid? Fifteen cents each. We can split it after school."

I noticed Mary was listening. She leaned over and held up one of her rolls. She wanted us to buy one.

Harry thought hard about what I had said. "I sure do miss Grandma's cookies. There's no home cooking when your oven is broken. And ours has been broken for five days now. Who knows how long it will take to save up the money to repair it?"

Mary raised her eyebrows. I

immediately turned my back to her. I didn't want Harry to see she was eavesdropping. Harry still wanted to keep his family problem a secret.

"Okay." Harry reached into his pants pocket and dumped everything onto the table. A handful of dirty coins, a bottle cap, and some cat hair. "Sixteen cents," Harry said. "That's all I have." He handed me fifteen cents, then returned the one lone penny and bottle cap to his pocket. He left the cat hairs on his desk.

Much to Mary's disappointment, I took Harry's pennies over to Sid's desk. I bought one cookie with Harry's fifteen cents plus the fifteen cents that I had in my pocket.

"That's my last cookie," Sid said. "My stepdad and I tripled the recipe, too."

I took the plastic Baggie with the good-sized chocolate chip cookie and walked over to the coat rack where my lunch box was. No one could see me back there, or what I was doing. So I took my time.

When I finally returned to my seat, Harry was smiling from ear to ear. He was probably thinking about eating his half of that delicious cookie after school.

"Boys and girls," Miss Mackle said, "it's time to put your money into one of the three donation jars. Please line up by my desk."

Harry tapped me on the shoulder. "Hey, Doug. Did you put our cookie in your lunchbox?"

I waited for Mary to go to the end of the line. I didn't want her to hear what I was going to say. When the coast was clear, I looked my buddy square in the eye. "Sorry, Harry, I couldn't help myself. I ate the whole thing."

"You *what*?" Harry replied.

"Ate it."

"But . . . that was supposed to be *our* cookie. I gave you my fifteen cents."

"Well, it's gone now."

"You stole that money from me! It was mine. My life savings!" Harry objected. His nose was in my face.

I stared right into Harry's brown eyeballs.

"Isn't that what you're doing with the Girl Scout money?" I whispered. "Taking something that's not yours?"

Harry suddenly leaned back. "How could you do that to me, Douglas?"

Douglas? That was new. He had never called me that before.

"You're a thief!" Harry snarled. "You stole my half of the chocolate chip cookie!" As soon as those words came out of his mouth, he looked away.

Neither of us said anything more. I just looked out the window and scowled.

When Mary returned to her seat, she was frowning, too.

I took my jar of coins to the teacher's desk and stood behind Dexter. He was humming an Elvis tune, "I'm All Shook Up."

That's for sure, I thought. I felt all
shook up. I had done my horrible deed.
And for what? I glanced back at Harry.
He was still sitting in his chair, fuming
with anger.

Ida dumped her earnings into the GSUSA jar. "Twelve dollars and fifty cents!" she said proudly.

ZuZu and Song Lee dropped their change into the UNICEF jar. "Twelve dollars and fifty cents, too," Song Lee said.

"Fifteen dollars and twenty-five cents," ZuZu added.

Dexter and Sidney poured their money into the ASPCA jar.

"I earned ten dollars by selling hand-made Elvis bookmarks! " Dexter said.

"I earned so much money I couldn't count it all!" Sidney bragged.

I put my eight dollars and seventy-five cents into the ASPCA jar, too. Harry got his cat, the Goog, from the animal shelter. I was glad they rescued stray cats like him.

"Wonderful!" Miss Mackle exclaimed. "Has everyone come up?"

Mary pointed to Harry. "He hasn't. Harry's the last one!"

I couldn't look at Harry anymore. I just stared at the three jars on Miss Mackle's desk. The Girl Scout jar had the least money. That's probably why Mary was frowning.

I heard Harry's chair moving and his footsteps. He was right behind me. I stepped aside. All eyes were on Harry.

How the Cookie Crumbled

Everyone watched Harry dump the money from his baby food container into the Girl Scout jar. "Seven dollars and fifty-five cents," he said.

And then he did something else.

Harry pulled out his brown coin purse, unzipped it, and shook all the change into the Girl Scout jar! "And seven dollars and fifty-five cents more," he mumbled.

Mary was jumping up and down. The three jars were just about even now.

I let out the biggest sigh. Harry couldn't do it after all! I started clapping. Everyone joined in with me.

Miss Mackle stood up from her desk. "Yes! You all did such a great job. Just look how full these donation jars are!" The teacher clapped with us. "We'll count the money tomorrow in math," she added.

When the three o'clock bell rang, Harry made a beeline for the hallway. His grandma always waited for him at the top of the ramp in her red truck. I quickly grabbed my jacket and bag and headed for the door.

Mary was behind me. "Wait up!" she called. She was just getting her jacket off the hanger. She always zipped hers up so it wouldn't fall on the floor and get dirty.

I couldn't wait for her. I had to catch up with Harry. He was running now, so I did, too.

"Harry, wait!" I called out.

He kept running.

"Please wait up," I insisted.

Harry finally stopped at the bottom of the ramp. "What for?" he growled.

"I'm glad you couldn't do it," I said. "And I know you're mad."

Harry didn't say anything.

I opened up my lunch box and held up the plastic Baggie with the chocolate chip cookie inside. Harry immediately took a step back. "You didn't eat it?"

"No. I just said I did."

"You made me feel like I was being robbed!" Harry replied. "Like you stole my life savings."

"I had to," I said. "You were going to do that to someone else. The Girl Scouts!"

Harry paused. "I didn't know it felt like that."

"No fun, huh?" I said.

"No," Harry agreed. "It felt like the time Sidney smashed my spider with a rock."

I put my arm around Harry. I remembered Charlie the spider.

"I can't steal anything," Harry confessed. "Not even for Grandma."

I opened up the Baggie and broke the cookie in two. Then I gave half to Harry.

"Thanks, Dougo," he said. "You stopped me from being a thief."

"Well, actually our cookie did. It was a super cookie."

Harry looked at his half. "It doesn't leap tall buildings in a single bound, but it does fight crime. Thanks, super cookie," he said, and he gobbled it down.

I ate my half, too.

While Harry licked the chocolate off his fingers, I looked around for something to wipe my hands on. That's when I saw Mary running toward us.

She was out of breath. "I want . . . to talk to . . . you, Harry."

Oh boy, I thought.

"I overheard you . . . talking to Doug . . . about your broken oven."

Harry was in a much better mood now. "You did? So, do you have a stove for me, Mare?" he joked.

"Well, actually, Harry, I do. I was wondering if you might want our old stove. It works fine. It's only a few years old, but it's the wrong color for our new kitchen. Mom was wondering what to do with it. So, if you want it—"

"Want it? Are you kidding!" Harry interrupted. "We'd love your old stove!"

Harry gave Mary a bear hug. Then he raced up the ramp, yelling, "Grandma, guess what?"

Mary looked embarrassed. But I didn't care, I gave her a hug, too. She really showed Harry how friends can help.

"Eweyee!" she groaned. "You guys got chocolate on my jacket."

"Ooops!" I tried not to laugh.

Suddenly Harry hollered from his truck. "Thank you, Mare! My grandma will call your mom!" And they drove off with the window down. I could see Harry's big toothy smile as he waved back at us.

Sidney's Delicious Chocolate Chip Cookie Recipe

What you need:

   2¼ cups flour
   1 teaspoon baking soda
   1 teaspoon salt
   2 sticks (1 cup) softened butter
   1 cup brown sugar
   ½ cup white sugar
   2 large eggs
   *2 tablespoons imitation vanilla (cheaper and
     it's just as good)*
   2 cups semi-sweet chocolate chips

1. Ask an adult to help you.
2. Preheat oven to 375 degrees.
3. Combine flour, baking soda, and salt in one bowl. Set aside.
4. Mix butter and sugars in a larger bowl. Beat until creamy.
5. Add eggs and vanilla. Beat well.
6. Stir in flour mixture.
7. Add chocolate chips.
8. Drop by tablespoon onto ungreased cookie sheet. Cook 11 minutes.

Makes 30 good-sized cookies. (You can split one and share it with a friend.)

Tip: Best if eaten warm. The next day, just microwave the cookie for 10 seconds.